Ruby
the Red
Fairy

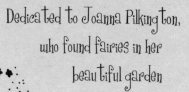

Dedicated to Joanna Pilkington,
who found fairies in her
beautiful garden

Special thanks to
Narinder Dhami

ISBN 0-439-73861-X

Copyright © 2003 by Working Partners Limited.

Illustrations copyright © 2003 by Georgie Ripper.

All rights reserved. Published by Scholastic Inc., 557 Broadway, New York, NY 10012, by arrangement with Working Partners Limited.

SCHOLASTIC, LITTLE APPLE, and associated logos are trademarks and/or registered trademarks of Scholastic Inc.

12 11 10 9 8 7 6 5 4 3 2 1   5 6 7 8 9 10/0

Printed in the U.S.A.

Ruby
the Red
Fairy

by Daisy Meadows
illustrated by Georgie Ripper

A
LITTLE APPLE
PAPERBACK

SCHOLASTIC INC.

New York   Toronto   London   Auckland   Sydney
Mexico City   New Delhi   Hong Kong   Buenos Aires

The
Fairyland
Palace

Maze

Forest

Orchard

Black
Pot

Meadow

Tower

Beach

Tide pools

Rainspell Island

Shells

Cold winds blow and thick ice forms,
I conjure up this fairy storm.
To seven corners of the human world
the Rainbow Fairies will be hurled!

I curse every part of Fairyland,
with a frosty wave of my icy hand.
For now and always, from this day,
Fairyland will be cold and gray!

Contents

The End of the Rainbow

Chapter 1

"Look, Dad!" said Rachel Walker. She pointed across the blue-green sea at the rocky island ahead of them. The ferry was sailing toward it, dipping up and down on the rolling waves. "Is that Rainspell Island?" she asked.

Her dad nodded. "Yes, it is," he said, smiling. "Our vacation is about to begin!"

The waves slapped against the side
of the ferry as it bobbed up and down
on the water. Rachel felt her heart
thump with excitement. She could see
white cliffs and emerald-green fields on
the island. Even golden sandy beaches,
with tide pools here and there.

Suddenly, a few fat raindrops
plopped down onto Rachel's head.
"Oh!" she gasped, surprised. The sun
was still shining.

Rachel's mom grabbed her hand.
"Let's get under cover," she said,
leading Rachel inside.

"Isn't that strange?" Rachel said.
"Sunshine *and* rain!"

"Let's hope the rain stops before we
get off the ferry," said Mr. Walker.
"Now, where did I put that map of
the island?"

Rachel looked out of the
window. Her eyes
opened wide.

A girl was standing
alone on the deck.
Her dark hair was
wet with raindrops,
but she didn't seem
to care. She just
stared up at the sky.

Rachel looked over at her mom and dad. They were busy studying the map. So Rachel slipped back outside to see what was so interesting.

And there it was.

In the blue sky, high above them, was the most amazing rainbow that Rachel had ever seen. One end of the rainbow stretched far out to sea. The other seemed to fall somewhere on Rainspell Island. All of the colors were bright and clear.

Red
Orange
Yellow
Green
Blue
Indigo
Violet

"Isn't it perfect?" the dark-haired girl whispered to Rachel.

"Yes, it is," Rachel agreed. "Are you going to Rainspell on vacation?"

The girl nodded. "We're staying for a week," she said. "I'm Kirsty Tate."

Rachel smiled as the rain began to stop. "I'm Rachel Walker. We're staying at Mermaid Cottage," she added.

"Oh! We're at Dolphin Cottage," said Kirsty. "Do you think we might be close to each other?"

"I hope so," Rachel replied. She had a feeling she was going to like Kirsty.

Kirsty leaned over the rail and looked down into the shimmering water. "The ocean looks really deep here, doesn't it?" she said. "There might even be mermaids down there, watching us right now!"

Rachel stared at the waves. She saw something that made her heart skip a beat. "Look!" she said. "Is that a mermaid's hair?" Then she laughed when she saw that it was just seaweed.

"It could be a mermaid's necklace," said Kirsty, smiling. "Maybe she lost it when she was trying to escape from a wild sea monster."

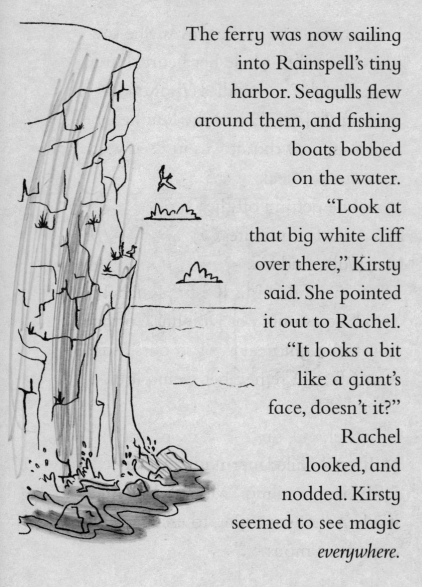

The ferry was now sailing into Rainspell's tiny harbor. Seagulls flew around them, and fishing boats bobbed on the water. "Look at that big white cliff over there," Kirsty said. She pointed it out to Rachel. "It looks a bit like a giant's face, doesn't it?" Rachel looked, and nodded. Kirsty seemed to see magic *everywhere*.

"There you are, Rachel!" called Mrs. Walker. Rachel turned around and saw her mom and dad coming out onto the deck. "We'll be getting off the ferry in a few minutes," Mrs. Walker added.

"Mom, Dad, this is Kirsty," Rachel said. "She's staying at Dolphin Cottage."

"That's right next door to ours," said Mr. Walker. "I remember seeing it on the map."

Rachel and Kirsty looked at each other and smiled.

"I'd better go and find *my* mom and dad," said Kirsty. She looked around. "Oh, there they are."

Kirsty's mom and dad came over
to say hello to the Walkers. Then the
ferry docked, and everyone began to
leave the boat.

"Our cottages are on the other side
of the harbor," said Rachel's dad,
looking at the map. "It's not too far."

Mermaid Cottage and Dolphin
Cottage were right next to the beach.
Rachel loved her bedroom, which was
high up in the attic. From the
window, she could see the waves
rolling onto the sand.

A shout from outside made Rachel look down. It was Kirsty. She was standing under the window, waving.

"Let's go and explore the beach!" Kirsty called.

Rachel dashed outside to join her.

Piles of seaweed lay on the sand, and there were tiny pink-and-white shells sprinkled everywhere.

"I love it here already!" Rachel shouted happily above the noise of the seagulls.

"Me, too," Kirsty said. She pointed up at the sky. "Look, the rainbow's still there."

Rachel looked up. The rainbow glowed brightly among the fluffy white clouds.

"Have you heard the story about the pot of gold at the end of the rainbow?" Kirsty asked.

Rachel nodded. "Yes, but that's just in fairy tales," she said.

Kirsty grinned. "Maybe. But let's go and find out for ourselves!"

"OK," Rachel agreed. "And maybe we can explore the island at the same time."

They rushed back to tell their parents
where they were going. Then Kirsty
and Rachel set off along a road behind
the cottages. It led them away from the
beach, across green fields, and toward
a small stretch of woods.

Rachel kept looking up at the rainbow. She was worried that it would start to fade now that the rain had stopped. But the colors stayed clear and bright.

"It looks like the end of the rainbow is over there," Kirsty said. "Come on!" And she hurried toward the trees.

The woods were cool and shady after being in the heat of the sun. Rachel and Kirsty followed a winding path until they came to a clearing. Then both girls stopped and stared.

The rainbow shone down onto the grass through a gap in the trees. Its colors sparkled and twinkled brightly.

And there, at the rainbow's end, lay an old, black pot.

A Tiny Surprise

"Look!" Kirsty whispered. "There really *is* a pot of gold!"

"It could just be a cooking pot," Rachel said doubtfully. "Some campers might have left it behind."

But Kirsty shook her head. "I don't think so," she said. "It looks really old."

Rachel stared at the pot. It was sitting on the grass, upside down.

"Let's have a closer look," said Kirsty. She ran to the pot and tried to turn it over. "Oh, it's heavy!" she gasped. She tried again, but the pot didn't move.

Rachel rushed to help her. They both pushed and pushed at the pot. This time it moved, but just a little.

"Let's try again." Kirsty said. "Are you ready, Rachel?"

Tap! Tap! Tap!

Rachel and Kirsty stared at each other.

"What was that?" Rachel gasped.

"I don't know," whispered Kirsty.

Tap! Tap!

"There it is again," Kirsty said. She looked down at the pot lying on the grass. "You know what? I think it's coming from inside this pot!"

Rachel's eyes opened wide. "Are you sure?" She bent down and put her ear to the pot. *Tap! Tap!* Then, to her amazement, Rachel heard a tiny voice.

"Help!" it called. "Help me!"

Rachel grabbed Kirsty's arm. "Did you hear that?" she asked.

Kirsty nodded. "Quick!" she said. "We have to turn the pot over, somehow!"

Rachel and Kirsty pushed at the pot as hard as they could. It began to rock from side to side on the grass.

"We're almost there!" Rachel cried.
"Keep pushing, Kirsty!"

The girls pushed with all their might.
Suddenly, the pot turned over and
rolled onto its side. Rachel and Kirsty
were taken by surprise. They both lost
their balance and landed on the grass
with a thump.

"Look!" Kirsty whispered, breathing
hard.

A small shower of sparkling red dust
had flown out of the pot.
Rachel and Kirsty gasped
with surprise. The dust
hung in the air above
them. And there, right in
the middle of the glittering
cloud, was a tiny, winged girl.

Rachel and Kirsty watched in wonder
as the tiny girl fluttered in the sunlight.
Her delicate wings sparkled with all the
colors of the rainbow.

"Oh, Rachel!" Kirsty whispered.
"It's a fairy. . . ."

Fairy Magic

The fairy flew over Rachel's and Kirsty's
head. Her short, silky dress was the
color of ripe strawberries. Red crystal
earrings glowed in her ears. Her golden
hair was braided with tiny red roses, and
she wore crimson slippers on her little feet.

The fairy waved her scarlet wand, and
a shower of sparkling red fairy dust

floated softly down to the ground. Where the dust landed, all kinds of red flowers appeared with a *pop!*

Rachel and Kirsty watched, openmouthed. This really and truly *was* a fairy.

"This is like a dream," Rachel said.

"I always believed in fairies," Kirsty whispered back. "But I never thought I'd ever *see* one!"

The fairy flew toward them. "Oh, thank you *so* much!" she called in a tiny voice. "I'm free at last!" She glided down and landed on Kirsty's hand.

Kirsty gasped. The fairy felt lighter and softer than a butterfly.

"I was beginning to think I'd *never* get out of that pot!" the fairy said.

Kirsty wanted to ask the fairy so
many things. But she didn't know
where to start.

"Tell me your names, quickly," said
the fairy. She fluttered up into the air
again. "There's so much to be done,
and we must get started right away."

Rachel wondered what the fairy meant. "I'm Rachel," she said.

"And I'm Kirsty," said Kirsty. "But who are *you*?"

"I'm the Red Rainbow Fairy — but you can call me Ruby," the fairy replied.

"Ruby . . ." Kirsty breathed. "A Rainbow Fairy . . ." She and Rachel stared at each other in excitement. This really *was* magic!

"Yes," said Ruby. "And I have six sisters: Amber, Sunny, Fern, Sky, Inky, and Heather. One for each color of the rainbow, you see."

"What do Rainbow Fairies do?"
Rachel asked.

Ruby flew over and landed lightly on
Rachel's hand. "It's our job to put all the
different colors into Fairyland," she
explained.

"So why were you shut up inside
that old pot?" asked Rachel.

"And where are your sisters?" Kirsty
added.

Ruby's golden wings drooped. Her
eyes filled with tiny, sparkling tears.
"I don't know," she said. "Something
terrible has happened in Fairyland. We
really need your help!"

Fairies in Danger

Kirsty stared down at Ruby, sitting sadly on Rachel's hand. "Of course we'll help you!" she said.

"Just tell us how," added Rachel.

Ruby wiped the tears from her eyes. "Thank you!" she said. "But first I must show you the terrible thing that has

happened. Follow me — as quickly as you can!" She flew into the air, her wings shimmering in the sunshine.

Rachel and Kirsty followed Ruby across the clearing. The fairy danced ahead of them, glowing like a crimson flame. She stopped at a small pond under a weeping willow tree. "Look! I can *show* you what happened yesterday," she said.

Ruby flew over the pond and scattered another shower of

sparkling fairy dust with her tiny,
red wand. All at once, the
water lit up with a strange,
silver light. It bubbled and
fizzed, and then became
still. With wide eyes,
Rachel and Kirsty
watched as a picture
appeared in the
water. It was like
looking through
a window into
another land! "Oh,
Rachel, look!"
said Kirsty.
A river of the
brightest blue ran swiftly
past hills of the greenest green. Scattered

on the hillsides were red-and-white toadstool houses. And on top of the highest hill stood a silver palace with four pink towers.

The towers were so high, their points were almost hidden by the fluffy white clouds that floated past.

Hundreds of fairies were making their way toward the palace. Some were walking and others were flying. Rachel and Kirsty could see goblins, elves, and pixies, too. Everyone seemed very excited.

"Yesterday was the day of the Fairyland Midsummer Ball," Ruby explained. She flew over the pond and pointed with her wand at a spot in the middle of the scene. "There I am, with my Rainbow sisters."

Kirsty and Rachel looked closely at
where Ruby was pointing. They saw
seven fairies, each dressed prettily in
her own rainbow color. Wherever

they flew, they left a trail of fairy dust
behind them.

"The Midsummer Ball is *very*
special," Ruby went on. "And my
sisters and I are always in charge of
sending out invitations."

The front doors of the
palace slowly opened to the
sound of tinkling music.

"Here come King
Oberon and Queen
Titania," said Ruby. "The
Fairy King and Queen.
They are about to
begin the ball."

Kirsty and Rachel watched as
the king and queen stepped through the
doors. The king wore a splendid golden
coat and crown. His queen wore a silver

34

dress and a tiara that sparkled with diamonds. Everyone cheered loudly. After a while, the king signaled for quiet. "Fairies and friends," he began. "We are very glad to see you all here. Welcome to the Mid-summer Ball!"

The fairies clapped their hands and cheered again. A band of green frogs in purple suits started to play their instruments, and the dancing began.

Suddenly, a gray mist filled the room.
Kirsty and Rachel watched in alarm
as all the fairies started to shiver. Then
a loud, chilly voice shouted out, "Stop the
music!"

The band fell silent. Everyone looked
scared. A tall, bony figure was pushing
his way through the crowd. He was
dressed all in white, and there were tiny
icicles on his white hair and beard. But
his face was red and angry.

"Who's that?" Rachel asked with a
shiver. Ice had begun to form around
the edge of the pond.

"It's Jack Frost," said Ruby. She
shivered, too.

In the watery picture Jack Frost glared
at the seven Rainbow Fairies. "Why

wasn't I invited to the Midsummer Ball?"
he asked coldly.

The Rainbow Fairies gasped in
horror. . . .

Ruby looked up and smiled sadly at
Rachel and Kirsty. "Yes, we forgot to invite

Jack Frost," she said, and looked back at the pond.

They watched as the Fairy Queen stepped forward. "You are more than welcome, Jack Frost," she said. "Please stay and enjoy the ball."

But Jack Frost looked even more angry. "Too late!" he hissed. "You forgot to invite me!" He turned and pointed a thin, icy finger at the Rainbow Fairies.

"You will not forget this!" he went on.

"My spell will banish the Rainbow Fairies to the seven corners of the human world. From this day on, Fairyland will be without color — forever!"

Jack Frost's Spell

As Rachel and Kirsty kept watching the pond's surface, they saw Jack Frost cast his spell. A great, icy wind began to blow. It picked up the seven Rainbow Fairies and spun them up into the darkening sky. The other fairies could only watch in dismay.

Jack Frost turned to the king and queen. "Your Rainbow Fairies will be trapped far away. They will be all alone, and they will never return." With that, he walked away, leaving only a trail of icy footprints behind.

Quickly, the Fairy Queen stepped forward and lifted her silver wand. "Jack Frost's magic is very powerful. I cannot undo it completely," she shouted, as the wind howled and rushed around

her. "But I can guide the Rainbow Fairies to a place where they will be safe until they are rescued!"

The queen pointed her wand at the gray sky overhead. A black pot came spinning through the stormy clouds. It flew toward the Rainbow Fairies. One by one, the Rainbow Fairies tumbled into the pot.

"May this pot at the end of the rainbow keep our Rainbow Fairies together and safe," the queen called. "And take them to Rainspell Island!"

As Rachel, Kirsty, and Ruby watched, the pot flew out of sight. It disappeared behind a dark cloud. And the bright colors of Fairyland began to fade, until the beautiful land looked like an old black-and-white photograph.

"Oh, no!" Kirsty gasped. "All the color is gone." Then the image in the pond vanished.

"So the Fairy Queen cast her *own* spell!" Rachel said. She was bursting with questions. "She put you and your sisters in the pot, and sent you to Rainspell Island?"

Ruby nodded. "Our queen knew that

we would be safe here," she said. "We
know Rainspell well. It is a place full of
magic."

"But where are your sisters?" Kirsty
asked. "They were in the pot, too."

Ruby looked upset. "Jack Frost's magic
was very strong," she said. "The wind
from his spell blew my sisters right out of

the pot. We were still spinning through the sky, and all at once they were gone." Ruby shook her head. "I was at the bottom, so I was safe. But I was trapped when the pot landed upside down. In the dark, I was frightened and alone. My fairy magic wouldn't even work!"

"So are your sisters somewhere on Rainspell?" Kirsty asked.

Ruby nodded. "Yes, but I think they're scattered all over the island. I'm sure Jack Frost's spell has trapped them, too." She flew toward Kirsty and landed on her shoulder. "That's where you and Rachel come in."

"How?" Rachel asked.

"You found *me,* didn't you?" the fairy went on. "That's because you believe in magic." She flew from Kirsty's shoulder to Rachel's. "So, you could rescue my Rainbow sisters, too! Once we're together, we can bring color back to Fairyland again."

A Visit to Fairyland

"Of course we'll search for your sisters,"
Kirsty said quickly. "Won't we,
Rachel?"

Rachel nodded.

"Oh, thank you!" Ruby said happily.

"But we're only here for a week,"
Rachel said. "Will that be long enough?"

"We have to get started right away,"

said Ruby. "First, I must take you to
Fairyland to meet our king and
queen. They will be very pleased to
know that you are going to help me
find my sisters."

Rachel and Kirsty stared at Ruby.

"You're taking us to *Fairyland*?"
Kirsty gasped. She could hardly believe
her ears.

"But how will we get there?" Rachel
wanted to know.

"We'll fly," Ruby replied.

"But *we* can't fly!" Rachel pointed
out.

Ruby smiled. She whirled up into
the air over the girls' heads. Then
she swirled her wand above them.
Magic red fairy dust fluttered
down.

Rachel and Kirsty began to feel a bit
strange. Were the trees
getting bigger or were
they getting smaller?

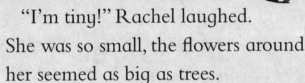

They were getting smaller!
Smaller and smaller and
smaller, until they were
the same size as Ruby.

"I'm tiny!" Rachel laughed.
She was so small, the flowers around
her seemed as big as trees.

Kirsty twisted around to look at her
back. She had wings —
shiny and delicate
as a butterfly's!
Ruby beamed
at them. "Now
you can fly," she
said. "Let's go."

Rachel twitched her shoulders. Her
wings fluttered, and she rose up into the
air. She felt quite wobbly at first. Flying
was not at all like walking!

"Help!" Kirsty yelled, as she shot up
into the air. "I'm not very good at this!"

"Come on," said Ruby, taking their
hands. "I'll help you." She led them up
out of the meadow.

From the air, Rachel looked down on
Rainspell Island. She could see the cottages
next to the beach, and the harbor.

"Where *is* Fairyland, Ruby?" Kirsty asked. They were flying higher and higher, up into the clouds.

"It's so far away that no human could ever find it," Ruby said.

They flew on through the clouds for a long, long time. But at last Ruby turned to them and smiled. "We're here," she said. "Luckily, while we're in Fairyland, no time passes in your world. No one will even know you were gone!"

As they flew down from the clouds, Kirsty and Rachel saw places they recognized from the pond picture: the palace, the hillsides with their toadstool houses, the river. But there were no bright colors now. Because of Jack Frost's spell, everything was a drab shade of gray.

A few fairies walked miserably across the hillsides. Their wings hung limply down their backs. No one even had the energy to fly.

Suddenly, one of the fairies glanced up into the sky. "Look!" she shouted. "It's Ruby. She's come back!"

At once, the fairies flew up toward
Ruby, Kirsty, and Rachel. They circled
around Ruby, looking much happier,
and asking lots of questions.

"Have you come from Rainspell,
Ruby?"

"Where are the other Rainbow
Fairies?"

"Who are your friends?"

"First, we must see the king and
queen. Then I will tell you
everything!" Ruby promised.

King Oberon and Queen Titania
were seated on their thrones. Their
palace was as gray and gloomy as
everything else in Fairyland. But they
smiled warmly when Ruby arrived with
Rachel and Kirsty.

"Welcome back, Ruby," the queen
said. "We have missed you."

"Your Majesties, I have found two
humans who believe in magic!" Ruby
announced. "These are my new friends,
Kirsty and Rachel."

Quickly, Ruby explained what had
happened to the other Rainbow Fairies.
She told everyone how Rachel and
Kirsty had rescued her.

"You have our thanks," the king
told them. "Our Rainbow Fairies are
very special to us."

"And will you help us to find Ruby's
Rainbow sisters?" the queen asked.

"Yes, we will," Kirsty said.

"But how will we know where to
look?" Rachel asked.

"The trick is not to look too hard,"
said Queen Titania. "Don't worry.
As you enjoy the rest of your vacation,
the magic you need to find each
Rainbow Fairy will find *you*. Just
wait and see."

King Oberon rubbed his beard
thoughtfully. "You have six days of
your vacation left, and six fairies to
find," he said. "A fairy each day.
That's a lot of fairy-finding. You
will need some special help." He
nodded at one of his footmen, a
plump frog in a buttoned-up jacket.

The frog hopped over to Rachel and
Kirsty and handed them each a tiny,
silver bag.

"The bags contain magic tools," the
queen told them. "Don't look inside

them yet. Open them only when you
really need to, and you will find
something to help you." She smiled at
Kirsty and Rachel.

"Look!" shouted another frog footman
suddenly. "Ruby is beginning to fade!"

Rachel and Kirsty looked at Ruby in
horror. The fairy was growing paler

before their eyes. Her lovely dress was
no longer red, but pink, and her golden
hair was turning white.

"Jack Frost's magic is still at work,"
said the king, looking worried. "We
cannot undo his spell until the Rainbow
Fairies are all together again."

"Quickly, Ruby!" urged the queen.
"You must return to Rainspell at once."

Ruby, Kirsty, and Rachel rose into the
air, their wings fluttering.

"Don't worry!" Kirsty called, as they
flew higher. "We'll come back with all
the Rainbow Fairies very soon!"

"Good luck!" called the king and queen.

Rachel and Kirsty watched Ruby
worriedly as they all flew off together. As
they got farther away from Fairyland,

Ruby's color began to return. Soon she was bright and sparkling again. The three girls reached Rainspell at last. Ruby led Rachel and Kirsty to the clearing in the woods, and they landed next to the old, black pot. Then Ruby scattered fairy dust over Rachel and Kirsty. There was a puff of glittering red smoke, and the two girls shot up to their normal size again. Rachel wriggled her shoulders. Yes, her wings were gone.

"Oh, I really *loved* being a fairy," Kirsty
said.

They watched as Ruby sprinkled her
magic dust over the old, black pot.

"What are you doing?" Rachel asked.

"Jack Frost's magic means that I can't
help you look for my sisters," Ruby
replied sadly. "If I try, I might fade away
completely. So I will wait for you here, in
the pot at the end of the rainbow."

Suddenly, the pot began to move. It rolled across the grass and stopped under the weeping willow tree. The tree's branches hung right down to the ground.

"The pot will be hidden under that tree," Ruby explained. "I'll be safe there."

"We'd better start looking for the other Rainbow Fairies," Rachel said to Kirsty. "Where shall we start?"

Ruby shook her head. "Remember what the queen said," she told them. "The magic will come to you." She flew over and sat on the edge of the pot. Then she pushed aside one of the willow branches and waved at Rachel and Kirsty. "Good-bye, and good luck!"

"We'll be back soon, Ruby," Kirsty promised.

"We're going to find all of your
Rainbow sisters," Rachel said firmly.
"Just you wait and see!"

Ruby is safely hidden in the
pot at the end of the rainbow.
Now Rachel and Kirsty must find
Amber the Orange Fairy!

They don't have much time!
Join their adventure in this special
sneak peek....

A Very Unusual Shell

"What a beautiful day!" Rachel
Walker shouted, staring up at the
blue sky. She and her friend Kirsty
Tate were running along Rainspell
Island's yellow, sandy beach. Their
parents walked a little way behind
them.

"It's a *magical* day," Kirsty added.
The two friends smiled at each other.

Rachel and Kirsty had come to
Rainspell Island for their vacations. But
they soon found out it really *was* a
magical place!

As they ran, they passed tide pools
that sparkled like jewels in the sunshine.

Rachel spotted a little *splash!* in one
of the pools. "There's something in
there, Kirsty!" She pointed. "Let's go
look."

The girls jogged over to the pool and
crouched down to see.

Kirsty's heart thumped as she gazed
into the crystal-clear water. "What is
it?" she asked.

Suddenly, the water rippled. A little
brown crab scuttled sideways across

the sandy bottom and disappeared under a rock.

Kirsty felt disappointed. "I thought it might be another Rainbow Fairy," she said.

"So did I." Rachel sighed. "Never mind. We'll keep looking."

"Of course we will," Kirsty agreed. Then she put her finger to her lips as their parents came up behind them. *"Shhh."*

Kirsty and Rachel had a big secret. They were helping to find the seven missing Rainbow Fairies. Jack Frost put a wicked spell on the fairies and trapped them on Rainspell Island. The Rainbow Fairies made Fairyland bright and colorful. Until they were all found, Fairyland would be dark and gray.

Rachel looked at the shimmering
blue sea. "Do you want to go
swimming?" she asked.

But Kirsty wasn't listening. She was
shading her eyes with her hand and
looking farther along the beach. "Look
over there, Rachel — by those rocks," she
said.

Then Rachel could see it, too —
something glittering and sparkling in the
sunshine. "Wait for me!" she called, as
Kirsty hurried down the beach.

When they saw what it was, the two
friends sighed in disappointment.

"It's just the wrapper from a
chocolate bar," Rachel said sadly. She
bent down and picked up the shiny
purple foil.

Kirsty thought for a moment. "Do you remember what the Fairy Queen told us?" she asked.

Rachel nodded. *"Let the magic come to you,"* she said. "You're right, Kirsty. We should just enjoy our vacation, and wait for the magic to happen."

Read the rest of

Amber *the Orange Fairy*

to find out what magic happens next....